Weekly Reader Children's Book Club Presents

Robert Kraus

Phil the Ventriloquist

HELLO

Greenwillow Books New York

This book is a presentation of Weekly Reader Books.
Weekly Reader Books offers book clubs for children from
preschool through high school. For further information write
to: **Weekly Reader Books,** 4343 Equity Drive, Columbus,
Ohio 43228.

Published by arrangement with Greenwillow Books.
Weekly Reader is a federally registered trademark of Field
Publications. Printed in the United States of America.

Watercolor paints, colored markers, and a
black pen were used for the full-color art.
The text type is Spartan Book.

First Edition   10 9 8 7 6 5 4 3 2 1

Library of Congress Cataloging-in-Publication Data
Kraus, Robert (date)
Phil the ventriloquist / by Robert Kraus.
p.   cm.
Summary: Phil's ability to throw his voice bothers his
parents until the night a burglar sneaks into the house.
ISBN 0-688-07987-3.   ISBN 0-688-07988-1 (lib. bdg.)
[1. Ventriloquism—Fiction.]   I. Title.
PZ7.K868Pf 1989
[E]—dc19   88-11   CIP   AC

Dear Parent:

Choosing a book for the Weekly Reader Book Club means finding one that kids will want to read over and over again. Although there are nearly 4,500 new children's books published every year, not all of them meet our criteria. A potential offering must be a book that

- is a family favorite or a contemporary book by an outstanding author and illustrator.

- is one we know children will like.

- fits the Weekly Reader tradition of wholesome recreational reading and enduring values.

Like many of our selections, *Phil the Ventriloquist* has been tested in local schools, libraries, and day care programs. And the vote is unanimous: Kids love this book! In fact, in a recent national survey children selected *Phil the Ventriloquist* as one of their favorite books. Subsequently, the book was given the International Reading Association's Children's Choice Award. Every time we share this book with children, they ask for it to be read twice, sometimes three times.

Robert Kraus's breezy style is one that kids will recognize from the many books he has created. *Phil the Ventriloquist* has the perfect blend of art and text, and Kraus's storytelling has never been funnier or more satisfying.

We hope you and your child enjoy this book.

Sincerely,

Fritz J. Luecke

Fritz J. Luecke
Executive Editor
Weekly Reader Books

For Parker

Phil was a ventriloquist.

He could throw his voice here.

He could throw his voice there.

Once, he threw his
voice into a trunk.

He could make trees talk.

Or so it seemed.

"Phil is getting on my nerves,"
said his father.

"Today he made my chair say
'Don't sit on me!'"

Phil's mother was upset, too.
He made some eggs she
was scrambling say
"Don't scramble me!"

And when she was
squeezing oranges
he made an orange scream
"Don't squeeze me!"

"We've got to do something,"
said Phil's parents.

So they went to a magic shop
and bought him
a ventriloquist's dummy.

But Phil wasn't interested
in the dummy.

It was more fun
to make his
father's shoes sing

and his mother's hat tell jokes.

"We can't take him anywhere,"
said Phil's father.
"He'll embarrass us."

"What will the neighbors say?"
cried Phil's mother.

Then one night a burglar
came in through a window.

Phil heard a noise
and woke up.

He crept downstairs.
He made his father's chair say
"Cheeze it, the cops!"
He made a bowl of fruit say
"Stick 'em up!"

He made a lamp say
"You're under arrest."
He made a picture on the wall
say "Crime does not pay."

The burglar was so frightened
he jumped back out of the window

and ran off.

Just then Phil's father came
downstairs with a baseball bat.

"Relax," Phil made the baseball
bat say. "Phil's chased
the burglar away."

Phil's mother came downstairs.
"Phil's a hero," she said when
she heard what happened.

"Phil's got talent,"
Phil's father said,
"and he got it from me."

They all went into the kitchen
to have cookies and milk.

"It's lucky we have a ventriloquist in the family," said Phil's mother.

"Three cheers for Phil!"
said the carton of milk.